The Woman I Am

Picas Series 8

Canadä

The Publisher gratefully acknowledges the support of
the Canada Council for the Arts for our publishing program.
The Publisher acknowledges the support of the Ontario Arts Council.
The Publisher gratefully acknowledges the financial support of the Book
Publishing Industry Development Program (BPIDP).

Dorothy Livesay

The Woman I Am

Guernica
Toronto·Buffalo·Lancaster (U.K.)
2000

First published in a different version by Press Porcépic in 1977.
First edition by Guernica Editions in 1991.
Second Edition.
Printed in Canada.
Typeset by Selina.

Antonio D'Alfonso, editor
Guernica Editions Inc.,
P.O. Box 117, Station P, Toronto (ON), Canada M5S 2S6
2250 Military Rd, Tonawanda, N.Y. 14150-6000 U.S.A.
Gazelle, Falcon House, Queen Square, Lancaster, LA1 1RN U.K.

Legal Deposit – 4th Quarter
National Library of Canada.
Library of Congress Catalog Card Number: 98-74235
Canadian Cataloguing in Publication Data
Livesay, Dorothy, 1909-1996
The Woman I Am
2 nd. ed.
(Picas series ; 8)
Originally publ.: Erin, Ont.: Porcépic Press, 1977;
Montréal, Guernica, 1991.
ISBN 1-55071-088-5
I. Title. II. Series.
PS8523.I82W6 2000 C811'.52 C98-901063-5
PR9199.3.L48W65 2000

Contents

1926-1971

FIVE POEMS FOR ALAN CRAWLEY

1887-1975

1971-1975

1975-1977

The Woman I Am

For my daughter, Marcia Hays

Interrogation

If I come unasked
Will you mind?
Will you be there,
Ready?

If I come unasked
Will you be kind,
Your look fair,
Steady?

If I come unasked
Will it be
As if a meadowlark
Suddenly
Startled you as you worked
And you smiled,
But were not disturbed –
Scarce thinking, even,
Of the bird or its heaven?

If I come unasked
Will you forget
What you ever learned
Of etiquette?

The Difference

Your way of loving is too slow for me.
For you, I think, must know a tree by heart
Four seasons through, and note each single leaf
With microscopic glance before it falls –
And after watching soberly the turn
Of autumn into winter and the slow
Awakening again, the rise of sap,
Then only will you cry: "I love this tree!"

As if the beauty of the thing could be
Made lovelier or marred by any mood
Of wind, or by the sun's caprice; as if
All beauty had not sprung up with the seed –
With such slow ways you find no time to love
A falling flame, a flower's brevity.

Climax

My heart is stretched on wires,
Tight, tight.
Even the smallest wind,
However light,
Can set it quivering –
And simply a word of yours,
However slight,
Could make it snap.

Time

The thought of you is like a glove
That I had hidden in a drawer:
But when I take it out again
It fits; as close as years before.

Green Rain

I remember long veils of green rain
Feathered like the shawl of my grandmother –
Green from the half-green of the spring trees
Waving in the valley.

I remember the road
Like the one which led to my grandmother's house,
A warm house with green carpets,
Geraniums, a trilling canary
And shining horse-hair chairs;
And the silence, full of the rain's falling
Was like my grandmother's parlour
Alive with herself and her voice, rising and falling–
Rain and wind intermingled.

I remember on that day
I was thinking only of my love
And of my love's house.
But now I remember the day
As I remember my grandmother
I remember the rain as the feathery fringe of her shawl.

Comrade

Once only did I sleep with you;
A sleep and love again more sweet than I
Have ever known; without an aftertaste.
It was the first time; and a flower could not
Have been more softly opened, folded out.
Your hands were firm upon me: without fear
I lay arrested in a still delight –
Till suddenly the fountain in me woke.

My dear, it's years between; we've grown up fast
Each differently, each striving by itself.
I see you now a grey man without dreams,
Without a living, or an overcoat;
But sealed in struggle now, we are more close
Than if our bodies still were sealed in love.

Serenade for Strings

For Peter

I

At nine from behind the door
The tap tapping
Is furtive, insistent;
Recurrent, imperative
The I AM crying
Exhorting, compelling.
At eleven louder!
Wilderness shaking
Boulders uprolling
Mountains creating
And deep in the cavern
No longer the hammer
Faintly insistent
No longer the pickaxe
Desperate to save us
But minute by minute
The terrible knocking
God at the threshold!
Knocking down darkness
Battering daylight.

II

O green field
O sun soaked
On lavish emerald
Blade and sharp bud piercing
O green field
Cover and possess me
Shield me in brightness now
From the knocking
The terrible knocking . . .

III

Again . . . Again . . . O again.
Midnight. A new day.
Day of days
Night of nights
Lord of lords.

Good Lord deliver us
Deliver us of the new lord
Too proud for prison
Too urgent for the grave . . .
Deliver us, deliver us.

O God the knocking
The knocking attacking
No breath to fight it
No thought to bridge it
Bare body wracked and writhing
Hammered and hollowed
To airless heaving.

IV

The clock now. Morning.
Morning come creeping
Scrublady slishing
And sloshing the waxway
And crying O world
Come clean
Clean for the newborn
The sun soon rising . . .

Rising and soaring
On into high gear . . .
Sudden knowledge!

Easy speedway
Open country
Hills low-flying
Birds up-brooding
Clouds caressing
A burning noon-day . . .

Now double wing-beat
Breasting body
Till cloudways open
Heaven trembles:
    And blinding
        searing
         terrifying
             cry!

The final bolt has fallen.
The firmament is riven.

V

Now it is done.
Relax. Release.
And here, behold your handiwork:
Behold – a man!

Abracadabra

For Peter at Halloween

In the wicked afternoon
When the witch is there
When night's downsnare
Swoops like a loon
Strafing the air
In the wicked afternoon

In the witty time of day
When the mind's at play
The cat's at call
The guitar off the wall
Wind holds sway
In the witty time of day

Then the witch will walk
Full of witty talk
And the cat will stalk
Tail high as a cock

The guitar in the room
Will fuss and fume
Strumming at the tune
For a wicked afternoon
And out in the park
Wind will unfrock
The autumn trees
And falling leaves
Shiver with shock.

And time with his
Weaving, wailing horn
Shivers my timbers

Shatters my corn:
Little boy blue
Blows a blue tune
On a wicked afternoon.

The Mother

She cannot walk alone. Must set her pace
To the slow count of grasses, butterflies,
To puppy's leap, the new bulldozer's wheeze
To Chinese fishman, balancing his pole.

She cannot think alone. Words must be
Poised to the smaller scope, immediates
Of wagon's broken wheel, a battered knee,
The sun's high promise for a day of play.

And when the active hours are gone, it's still
Her lot to busily bestir herself
With knots and nooses, all the slough and slips
Of day. When evening's seal is set she must

Have chosen here to stay. To sit, to hear
The day's confessions eased from tired tongue,
To soothe the small lids down to drowsiness
Till childhood sleep perfumes the darkened room.

Easter

Painful the probing spring
pernicious for
those who refuse
growth, for fear.

And is there fear
in each incisive thrust
of white shoot from the dark
cold kingdom of the loam?
And in each awkward wing
weaned from a leafy home?

Or is the human young alone
the unaccepting one
afraid to face the sun
or green fires of the bone?

V-J Day

It seemed a poor thing to do, to wed, when the Japanese
Had begun to gnaw their way through the Manchu plains,
When Spain cast a ballot, and was outraged, raped
In an olive grove, by a monastery wall.
It seemed no time for love, when the hands
Idled in empty pockets and coffee was five cents a cup.
It seemed no time to lie down in a clearing
At sundown, with the woodcutters gone, and the thrush's
Voice fluting the firs. But you said: "Have faith."
You said, "Only Hitler was in a hurry and his haste
Would one day be spent." So you said. And we wed.
Now it is eight years after, to the day, to the hour:
The wrath has devoured itself and the fire eaten the fire.
And again at sundown over the bird's voice, low
Over the firs fluted with evening I hear the Yangtse flow
And the rubble of Barcelona is this moss under my hand.

Variations on a Tree

I

Confined to a narrow place
This consciousness, the Word
Is my predicament to be
Separate, yet joined,
Single, yet twain,
Twined in the ancestry of roots
Yet roving in the upper space.

Or are there roots
Seeking to soak themselves in cloud
Crying to the Lord aloud
Stretching out for sustenance
Towards the sun's own countenance?
Invert the world: now see it roll
Lightly on my palms,
And I, immeasurably deep
Wading in pools of blue
Dance branches in eternity
Play football with the moon.

II

Tree falls in foam
On a far shore
Spilling its coins
On the green floor

An aspen bridge
The tightrope where
My childhood walks –
No room to spare.

But island gained
Was world well lost,
No seething heat,
No stiffening frost,

Into your arms
Tossed at last;
Branches of silence
Consign the past.

III

The tree is Ego, yet
Leaning towards another
With mystery the same;
These twain are brother.

And two together go
Into the forest, with intent
To love and grow;
Branches embraced and bent –

Brave pattern for
World's tottering wall;
A roof of hands
Against sky fall.

The Three Emilys

Emily Brontë, Emily Dickinson and Emily Carr

These women crying in my head
Walk alone, uncomforted:
The Emilys, these three
Cry to be set free –
And others whom I will not name
Each different, each the same.

Yet they had liberty!
Their kingdom was the sky:
They batted clouds with easy hand,
Found a mountain for their stand;
From wandering lonely they could catch
The inner magic of a heath –
A lake their palette, any tree
Their brush could be.

And still they cry to me
As in reproach –
I, born to hear their inner storm
Of separate man in woman's form
I yet possess another kingdom, barred
To them, these three, this Emily.
I move as mother in a frame,
My arteries
Flow the immemorial way
Towards the child, the man;
And only for brief span
Am I an Emily on mountain snows
And one of these.

And so the whole that I possess
Is still much less –

They move triumphant through my head:
I am the one
Uncomforted.

Epithalamium for Susan

Susan Allison, née Moir, who on her wedding night rode over the Hope-Princeton Trail to become "the first white woman of the Similkameen." Later the Allisons settled at Westbank on Lake Okanagan.

I

A name beats in my blood –
Similkameen!
River of cool caress
and sudden flood
over whose veins we rode
gay and rough-shod.

That was a bridal ride
into Similkameen
with Indian as guide
and lover by my side
over the Skagit bluff
September scorched
where mountains opened up
mirror on mirror
each a reflection of
the other's face –
message of love
from a further place.
We moved from frame to frame
into a land unmapped
and crying for a name;
our horses' hooves
beat a new alphabet

on mountainside and lake
calling out:
Skagit, Cedars, Cayuse Creek:
the trail was tried!

II

At night the tales I heard
from Yacum-Tecum and I-cow-mas-ket
around our campfire, stirred
from centuries lost
from caves of silence drawn –
of satyr, shuswap and of giants born
invisible, save to the Indian eye –
those fiery myths breathed life into the stones
and made the boulders move
(I dared to touch one, and let loose a cry:
I was burned through).

III

So it was true, as you
long afterwards accused:
I did not give myself to you.
For on that wedding-night
I was a girl bound over to the hills,
my essence pierced with arrows of night air –
tang of sagebrush and the clear
perfume of pine.
No linen sheets for marriage-bed, but I
lay soft on "mountain feathers" – spruce,
mouth stained with huckleberry juice;
as epithalamium I heard
the deep drum's beat, the guttural song
sounding in my blood and bone:
the river pounding loud and long
calling me home – Similkameen!

Bartok and the Geranium

She lifts her green umbrellas
Towards the pane
Seeking her fill of sunlight
Or of rain;
Whatever falls
She has no commentary
Accepts, extends,
Blows out her furbelows,
Her bustling boughs;

And all the while he whirls
Explodes in space,
Never content with this small room:
Not even can he be
Confined to sky
But must speed high and higher still
From galaxy to galaxy,
Wrench from the stars their momentary notes
Steal music from the moon.

She's daylight
He is dark
She's heaven-held breath
He storms and crackles
Spits with hell's own spark.

Yet in this room, this moment now
These together breathe and be:
She, essence of serenity,
He in a mad intensity
Soars beyond sight
Then hurls, lost Lucifer,
From heaven's height.

And when he's done, he's out:
She leans a lip against the glass
And preens herself in light.

Other

I

Men prefer an island
with its beginning ended:
undertone of waves
trees overbended.

Men prefer a road
Circling shell-like
convex and fossiled
forever winding inward.

Men prefer a woman
limpid in sunlight
held as a shell
on a sheltering island . . .

Men prefer an island.

II

But I am mainland
O I range
from upper country to the inner core:
from sageland brushland marshland
to the sea's floor.

Show me an orchard where I have not slept
a hollow where I have not wrapped
the sage about me and above the still
stars clustering
over the ponderosa pine the cactus hill.

Tell me a time
I have not loved,
a mountain left unclimbed:
a prairie field
where I have not furrowed my tongue,
nourished it out of the mind's dark places;
planted with tears unwept
and harvested as friends   as faces.

O find me a dead-end road
I have not trodden
a logging road that leads the heart away
into the secret evergreen of cedar roots
beyond sun's farthest ray –
then, in a clearing's sudden dazzle
there is no road; no end; no puzzle.

But do not show me! For I know
the country I caress:
a place where none shall trespass
none possess:
a mainland mastered
from its inaccess.

Men prefer an island.

Lament

For J.F.B.L.

What moved me, was the way your hand
Lay in my hand, not withering,
But warm, like a hand cooled in a stream
And purling still; or a bird caught in a snare
Wings folded stiff, eyes in a stare,
But still alive with the fear,
Heart hoarse with hope –
So your hand, your dead hand, my dear.

And the veins, still mounting as blue rivers,
Mounting towards the tentative finger-tips,
The delta where four seas come in –
Your fingers promontories into colourless air
Were rosy still – not chalk (like cliffs
You knew in boyhood, Isle of Wight):
But blushed with colour from the sun you sought
And muscular from garden toil;
Stained with the purple of an iris bloom,
Violas grown for a certain room;
Hands seeking faience, filagree,
Chinese lacquer and ivory –
Brussels lace; and a walnut piece
Carved by a hand now phosphorous.

What moved me, was the way your hand
Held life, although the pulse was gone.
The hand that carpentered a children's chair,
Carved out a stair
Held leash upon a dog in strain
Gripped wheel, swung sail,
Flicked horse's rein
And then again

Moved kings and queens meticulous on a board,
Slashed out the cards, cut bread, and poured
A purring cup of tea;

The hand so neat and nimble
Could make a tennis partner tremble,
Write a resounding round
Of sonorous verbs and nouns –
Hand that would not strike a child, and yet
Could ring a bell and send a man to doom.

And now unmoving in this Spartan room
The hand still speaks:
After the brain was fogged
And the tight lips tighter shut,
After the shy appraising eyes
Relinquished fire for the sea's green gaze –
The hand still breathes, fastens its hold on life;
Demands the whole, establishes the strife.

What moved me, was the way your hand
Lay cool in mine, not withering;
As bird still breathes, and stream runs clear –
So your hand; your dead hand, my dear.

Widow

No longer any man needs me
nor is the dark night of love
coupled

But the body is relentless, knows
its need
must satisfy itself without the seed
must shake in dreams, fly up the stairs
backwards.

In the open box in the attic
a head lies, set sideways.

This head from this body is severed.

On Looking into Henry Moore

I

Sun   stun me   sustain me
turn me to stone:
Stone   goad me   and gall me
urge me to run.

When I have found
passivity in fire
and fire in stone
female and male
I'll rise alone
self-extending and self-known.

II

The message of the tree is this:
aloneness is the only bliss

Self-adoration is not in it
(Narcissus tried, but could not win it)

Rather, to extend the root
tombwards, be at home with death

But in the upper branches know
a green eternity of fire and snow.

III

The fire in the farthest hills
is where I'd burn myself to bone:
clad in the armour of the sun
I'd stand anew alone

Take off this flesh   this hasty dress
prepare my half-self for myself:
one unit   as a tree or stone
woman in man   and man in womb.

After Grief

Death halves us:
every loss
divides
our narrowness
and we are less.

But more:
each losing's an encore
of clapping hands
dreaming us on;
the same scene played once more
willing us grander than
we were:
no dwarf *menines*
but kings and queens.

And still, some say
death raises up
gathers the soul strong-limbed
above the common tide
to catch a glimpse
(over world's wailing wall)
of an exultant countryside.

Ballad of Me

I

Misbegotten
born clumsy
bursting feet first
then topsy turvy
falling downstairs;
the fear of
joy of
falling.

Butterfingers
father called it
throwing the ball
which catch as catch can
I couldn't.

Was it the eyes' fault
seeing the tennis net
in two places?
the ball flying, falling
space-time team-up?

What happened was:
the world, chuckling sideways
tossed me off
left me wildly
treading air
to catch up.

II

Everyone expected guilt
even I –
the pain was this:
to feel nothing.

Guilt? for the abortionist
who added one more line
to his flat perspective
one more cloud of dust
to his bleary eye?

For the child's
onlie begetter
who wanted a daughter?
He'll make another.

For the child herself
the abortive dancer?

No. Not for her
no tears.
I held the moon in my belly
nine months' duration
then she burst forth
an outcry of poems.

III

And what fantasies do you have?
asked the psychiatrist
when I was running away from my husband.
Fantasies? Fantasies?
Why surely (I might have told him)
all this living
is just that

every day dazzled
gold coins falling
    through fingers
So I emptied my purse for the doctor
See! nothing in it
but wishes.
He sent me back home
to wash dishes.

IV

Returning further now
to childhood's *Woodlot*
I go incognito
in sandals, slacks
old sweater
and my dyed
hair

I go disarrayed
my fantasies
twist in my arms
ruffle my hair

I go wary
fearing to scare
the crow

        No one remembers Dorothy
        was ever here.

Postscript

For Phyllis Webb

There was a man here, this morning
from Mars, looking us over.
–Why do you stay?
he said.
And I was at pains to set it
down
and ask myself

Why not go?

Walk along the wave-bent shore
wind-twisted roots
and as the tide and I
measure our distances
stalk out, barefoot
a shrunken, bowed and heavy-bellied form
skirt hugging the knees
into the cold salt seeking my warm blood?

Why not go?

The trouble is, it comes soon enough,
I told him:
we, down here, are constantly aware
that the moment lies lurking
between one drink and another
one shout and another
one kiss   one blow
and a heart's beat.

So, why care?

– But I don't see why, he began.
You mean, what's the sense in waiting?
He nodded, all frightening fascination
his eyes tearing mine from their sockets.
So I had to find it
to dig frantic the pocket of memory
pull out all the irrelevances
and lay them on the table.

– What's this? he cried, seizing
a handful of hair.
– A girl's first golden sowing
cropped at two years old –
softer than down
but gone now! coarse hair, black
so wiry you'd never know.
It's the softness, I said, the gold –
is why.

And a marble: hard,
a world half-sea, half-sun
red at the rim.
– What's that to you? he said.
– A boy's game, I cried
playing with the world
under a cherry-tree
under the moon's tide.
For a marble eye
I'd stay.

Then he found the bowl of a pipe
pock-marked with tobacco
smelling of human breath
dead fires.
– You care for this?

– It was his view of mountains:
he puffed them into his pipe
and out again.
Now I can recognize
mountains.

Anything else?
No. Not unless –
unless counting counts.
A cat can count her kittens
up to five.
After that
she's lost.
I count the man
the boy, the girl
and myself –
– and last?
– I count my verse.

That's counted you out, he said.

Woman Waylaid

For "Jim" Watts Lawson

Having to have
heat
for the cool evenings
by the lake

is having   to search
allmornings paths
stumbling   on ants' nests
interrupting traffic
for five newborn
blue butterflies
discovering   violets
the pale open-to-sky
kind   no scent
meeting head-on
the lion-headed
dandyman

having to have
heat
return empty –
handed
to face
pot-bellied stove
its greed:

it gapes
for leaf for twig for bark for tree
and cannot be fed

on flowers.

Eve

Beside the highway
at the motel door
      it roots
the last survivor of a pioneer
      orchard
miraculously still
      bearing.
A thud   another apple fall
      I stoop   and   O
that scent   gnarled ciderish
      with sun in it
that woody pulp
      for teeth and tongue
      to bite and curl around
that spurting juice
      earth sweet!

In fifty seconds, fifty summers sweep
      and shake me –
I am alive!   can stand
      up   still
hoarding this apple
      in my hand.

The Unquiet Bed

The woman I am
is not what you see
I'm not just bones
and crockery

the woman I am
knew love and hate
hating the chains
that parents make

longing that love
might set men free
yet hold them fast
in loyalty

the woman I am
is not what you see
move over love
make room for me

The Touching

I

Caress me
shelter me now
    from the shiver
of dawn
"the coldest hour"

pierce me again
    gently
so the penis completing
    me
rests in the opening
    throbs
and its steady pulse
    down there
is my second heart
    beating

II

Light nips the darkness
        a white frost
    breaking in ripples
        on a dark ground
    like light your kisses hover
        touching my nipples
    under the cover

III

Each time you come
      to touch caress
me
      I'm born again
            deaf   dumb
each time
      I whirl
            part of some mystery
I did not make or earn
that seizes me
      each time
I drown
      in your identity
I am not I
      but root
            shell
                  fire
each time you come
I tear through the womb's room
      give birth
and yet   alone
      deep in the dark
      earth
I am the one   wrestling
the element re-born.

The Taming

Be woman. You did say me, be
woman. I did not know
the measure of the words

until a black man
as I prepared him chicken
made me listen:
– No, dammit.
Not so much salt.
Do what I say, woman:
just that
and nothing more.

Be woman. I did not know
the measure of the words
until that night
when you denied me darkness,
even the right
to turn in my own light.

Do as I say, I heard you faintly
over me fainting:
be woman.

Dream

Sudden
a sceptred bird
swept through the window
into the blue room
and dazzled me

I swam in light –
he stooped
and pecked out my eyes
    I move in darkness now
    fumbling the walls
    trying to remember
    blue
        (I have closed the window
        and the sun falls cold
        through glass)

The Uninvited

Always a third one's there
where any two are walking out
along a river-bank   so mirror-still
sheathed in sheets
of sky   pillows of cloud –
their footprints crunch the hardening earth
their eyes delight in trees   stripped clean
winter-prepared
with only the rose-hips red
and the plump fingers of sumach

And always between the two
(scuffling the leaves, laughing
and fingers locked)
goes a third lover   his or hers
who walked this way with one or other   once
flung back the head   snapped branches of dark pine
in armfuls   before snowfall
    I walk beside you
    trace
    a shadow's shade
    skating on silver
    hear
    another voice
    singing under ice

The Snow Girl's Ballad

I should have let you lay me in the snow
then lift me back
so that my body's trace
might still be there
come spring
a power in the grass
my bones
firing the stone
my eyes
anemone

O brightly would I lie
the body that you traced
with your fine fingers
the gaze entranced
from my garden place
up to your story window

I should have let you know
more things about me
and never let you find
a world within
without me.

Latter Day Eve

But supposing (only supposing)
it was God himself, not Satan
who held up the forbidden fruit
above her vision
(and not an apple – the biblical *fruit* –
but a cluster of cherries?)
He   an old roué   lusting
held up over her head
the glowing cherries
and it was Adam
young   virile   eager
who plucked one swiftly
and popped it into her mouth.
Ah, sweetness!
the sweetness of ripe cherry.

When they were ushered out
into a world of teeming traffic
demolition deluge
cranes screeching
scaffolds folding
yellow caterpillars churning up
the lost
the last dimension
she glued herself to a telephone pole
and panicked, hoarsely:
where are you,
Adam?
Adam, where are you?

At the motel desk
she held up her room-key
so he would surely
see

but his eyes gazed steadily past her
at some disappearing waitress
and she flashed the key
fruitlessly!

Look to the End

Respice ad finem, the Livesay motto

And if I hurt my knee
my good leg shows my poor leg
what to do

and if I hurt my arm
my good arm rubs my poor arm
into place

and if I hurt an eye
my good eye sees beyond the other's range
and pulls it onward   upward
into space

The sun's eye warms my heart
but if my good heart breaks
I have no twin
to make it beat again

Disasters of the Sun

I

O you old
gold garnered
incredible sun
sink through my skin
into the barren bone

If I'm real
I'm totem carved
with your splayed
scalpel

If I'm a person
the gods roar
in horrible surprised
masculinity

but if I'm a woman
paint me
with the beast stripes
assure me I am human

II

The world is round
it is an arm
around us
my fingers touching Africa
your hand
tilting Siberian trees
our thoughts
still as the tundra stones
awaiting footprints
bright between our bones
shines the invisible sun

III

Though I was certain
we recognized each other
I could not speak:
the flashing fire
between us
fanned no words

In the airport circle   where
the baggage tumbled
all my jumbled life
fumbled
to find the one sweet piece
the clothing stuffed and duffled
labelled mine

and over across the circle saw
your dark hair, piercing eyes
lean profile, pipe in mouth.

Incredibly, you move.
You seem to dance
and suddenly
you stand beside me, calm
without surprise:

I cannot tell
what country you are from
we recognize each other
and are dumb

your hand   your hand
tense on your pipe
your look   *a soft bomb*
behind my eyes

IV

My hands that used to be leaves
tender and sweet and soothing
have become roots
gnarled in soil

my hands
tender as green leaves
blowing on your skin
pulling you up
into joyous air
are knotted bones
whitening in the sun

V

During the last heat wave
a sunflower
that had stood up straight
outstaring the June
sun
wilted collapsed
under a pitiless July
sky

now in burning August
I close out the city
trembling under heat
the green trees visibly
paling –

I close and curtain off myself
into four walls
breezed by a fan
but the fan
fumes!

and suddenly it
BREAKS OFF   from the wall
whirls   across the room
to rip my forefinger.

I tell you
we live in constant
danger
under the sun   bleeding
I tell you

VI

Keep out
keep out of the way of
this most killing
northern sun
grower   destroyer

Sun, you are no goodfather
but tyrannical king:
I have lived sixty years
under your fiery blades
all I want now
is to grope for those blunt
moon scissors

VII

When the black sun's
gone down
connect me underground:
root tentacles
subterranean water

no more lovely man can be
than he with moon-wand
who witches water.

Five Poems for Alan Crawley
1887-1975

Nocturne

Countries are of the mind
and when you moved upon my land
your darkness ringed my light:
O landscape lovely, looped
with loping hills, wind-woven
landfall of love.

All my frozen years
snow drifting through bare birches
white-cowled cedar
and the black stream threading through ice –

All sultry summers run
barefooted through the crackling wood
flung upon rocks made skeleton
x-rayed by the raging sun –

All springs, wild crying with the wood's mauve bells
anemone, hepatica
breast against bark, the sap's ascent
burning the blood with bold green fire –

All autumns, solitary season
treading the leaves, treading the time:
autumns that stripped deception to the bone
and left me animal, alone –

All seasons were of light
stricken and blazing –

Only now the shout
of knowledge hurls, amazing:
O bind me with ropes of darkness,
blind me with your long night.

To Be Blind

To be blind
is to not-know
world's flow
is to live
so sensitive to sound
that meanings bound
    re-bound
and make non-sense

through the raw tingling
other senses
meanings fray out
there's no
consensus

To be blind
is to grope for
a   hand   an arm   a stick
sometimes a great hug
comes
and the blood hums . . .
but afterwards
words falter

To be blind
is to have a halter
around the neck
and friends' well-meaning
tugs
strangle one faster.

March 26

For Jean Crawley

She expired at one a.m.
the hospital voice said

in this month of spring's beginning
buds at my window   swollen
greenish   rose-streaked – pregnant

she expired
drew a great breath
out of her eighty years
of living

couldn't they call a spade a spade
I wanted to shout
couldn't they say
she died?

But perhaps the euphemism
fits you, Jean –
for always the conventional way
and the social techniques
of living
were your game:
you played it brilliantly

I know now
you would have chosen to die as you did
in a proper hospital bed
your loved one beside you
his hand curled
in the shell of yours

I know now
"the heart had run its course"
but the voice   the voice
incisive clear
rings on in memory's ear.
Hello?
Hello, my dear.

The Prisoner of Time

Caught and trapped
age has put you through its mangle
I see you now, just bits and pieces
of the old flare
sparks feebly hitting
the dry air

I hear you now
an echo across the valley
JOY . . . LIFE . . .
becoming oyoyoy . . . if . . .
I apprehend you now
brittle chips off the old block
trying to remember a name
a place
desperate to recall
the loved face

Better to die young?
flung
from garden into ocean?
O my dear
I remember your voice dancing
its mimetic motion
I remember your keen mind
cutting through ice and stone

All I can do now
is hold your hand
all I can say
is *tovarisch tovarisch*
we are not alone.

Every Woman You Loved

Every woman you loved
I am
but I am the only one left
now to come

At the hospital bed
I stand beside your spare form
stooping over
to kiss the bent brow
to hear you say
from your blind, deaf world
"Oh do not go away –
Stay. Stay!"

I seek for your palm
the grasp is firm
free and happy as always
pulsing, cogent
but no flesh there
nothing but its end,
bare bone – despair
earth's sufferance –
O my dear
my dear

How can we ever connect
the disappearing flesh
collapsing bone
with belief in the heart's everness
endlessly beating
its way home?

1971-1975

Why We Are Here

Some of us are here
because we were visited
at dawn
were given a third
ear

Some of us especially
are women
open
over receiving
into

Layton says
"The womb
is such a diminutive room
in which to lie"

But some of us are here
to say   *lie down*
children of men
lie down on the stiff brown stubble
at noon   the ice
melting to puddles
lie down at noon
on hard soil
singing with underground
water
lie down
and let our hands bear you as rivers
to the sea's room.

Some of us are here
as messages
because in the small womb
lies all the lightning.

Interiors

I am sitting in another house
by another window
a green plaid blanket
over my knees

There is a garden outside . . .
trees . . .
grass sloping to the river
as far as the eye sees

It is summer and winter
fall and spring
all in one view
breath-catching

It is time to go
and time to come
children springing into men
and old men dwindling
into green

I am listening for your step
and when you come, I fling
all old age off
am in your arms
enveloped by that home

And then your face
is other faces found
your voice
is other voices
scaling a new sound

Then all are gone . . .
The trees bow down
the river rises up
crashing against the pane:
those waters swamp the room
and bear me on.

Blue Wind

For Martha

Spirit of wind
blue skirt against blue-green grass
hair fair
straw-coloured
straight and prim
a coif   for skyblue eyes
staring amazed
at the wild
woods   fields
folding hills
ever yielding
ever flowering
earth

Spirit of wind
granddaughter
moving undaunted
round the bend
into the frightening
tight-drawn highways

Against these,
blow and burn!
contrive to comprehend
survive to sway
to the will of the wind.

Return to a Birthplace

Hi lady   lady
ladybird
the children cry
as you sedately
walk waylaid
(when you are fifty
        you don't feel any older
        said the mother
        dusting the pollen
        from her shoulder)
            fly away, fly away home

High lady   lady
feet first
gopher on the grass
then up, fly
tickle your toes
on tip-tops
of cottonwood
assess
the sky-blue
sea
with cloud sails scarfed
across the soil
where over the knuckle
of last year's cracks

and white whiskers of stubble
your tableland   spreads black . . .

Then let
new blades of wheat
grow a green fur
over the earth-bare
ribs

And fly!
on wings new grown
O lady   lady
skim high sky

When you come down

Where is your home?
Your house is on fire
Your children are gone

Aging

My body haunts me
thieves in on me at night
shattering sleep
with nameless pointless pains

Where do you ache?
The Chinese doctor's skill
might poise with needle
over my tossing form

but there's no
one still spot   no
one still time I'd swear:
The pain is here.

And every night
my fingers search the wound, the old
spine curvature, the creaking knees . . .
but tongues, the darting tongues
lick elsewhere, fan desire
until all yesterdays are gulfed
in freezing fire.

Parenthood

My child is like a stone
in wilderness
pick it up and rub it on the cheek
there's no response
or toss it down . . .
only a hollow sound
but hold it in the hand
a little time
it warms, it curves
softly into the palm:
even a stone takes on a pulse
in a warm hold.

For the New Year

Stamped in the throat
bird song
biologists say
is inevitable
as that beak, that eye
that red wing
is not *learned*
is born with the bird

Perhaps then there's another
dimension behind our learned
word patterns . . .
perhaps an infinite song
sways in our throats
yet to be heard?

The Cabbage

The doctor goes on handing out pills
that reduce me
from animal
to vegetable

Why couldn't he
implant some sunflower seeds
so at least I'd be able to see
over the fence?

For Rent

People have to live, I know that
explained the old Scotch body
from the rooms next door:
if they have a cough
they have to cough!
I can take that

but people don't have to shout all night
and play judo on the floor
so I can't get a stitch
of sleep

It's not people's morals I'm complaining about
. . . I know all about birds beasts and flowers . . .
that's not my business

It's how they don't care about the walls
and the creaking floors
and the paint falling down from the ceiling
onto my good rug

And I can’t pay anymore rent
than this

I’ve got nowhere to go.

Widow

The woman remembering
the man who died
that sweet connection
the woman sowing
nasturtium seed
planting geraniums
feels, waking at midnight
flowers growing out of her belly
rain falling on her thighs
the itch of nipples
pouting for kisses

The woman remembering
uses her hand to thrust
tries to recover
the heave and wrestle

but knows
it’s all play
and games
knows how memory
can never seal
that bond of flesh
body within body

Mathematics

I want to play the great game, darling
but only you can play it to perfection:
Much talk . . . no bed. Some talk . . . some bed
no talk . . . all bed;   and talk tomorrow.

I meant to play the great game, darling
and hold your bones deep to the root of one
I meant to play the great game, darling
but the heart for it   is gone.

Grandmother

O lovely raw red wild
outward turned
it's time to think of the blood
and the red searing

pale pale   the poets and poetasters
moving along the midnight mists
those riverbanks where girls
white flanked, never refuse,
yield all their mysteries

Give me instead
a small child noting
holly and rowan berry ripen
a small hand clasped

Who is there? What's that?
O, to survive
what must we do
to believe?
In the trees, my grandson.
In these roots. In these leaves.

Ice Age

For Laura Damania

In this coming cold
devouring our wheat fields
and Russia's
there'll be no shadow
nor sign of shadow
all cloud, shroud
endless rain
eternal snow

In this coming cold
which we have fashioned
out of our vain jet-pride,
the supersonic planes
will shriek destruction
upon the benign
yin yang
ancient and balanced universe

Worse than an animal
man tortures his prey
given sun's energy
and fire's blaze
he has ripped away
leaf
        bird
                flower
is moving to destroy
the still centre
heart's power.
Now who among us
will lift a finger
to declare *I am of God, good?*
Who among us
dares to be righteous?

Morning Rituals

I
Waking

It isn't morning:
the dark still lies
frozen upon her face
below my window

a siren cries

I have forgotten
the names of my lovers
but not their faces
not their bony frames

It isn't morning
and I have wakened
from a dream of one face
narrow   framed in sandy hair
unbeautiful
He talked more than he made love

Outside this window
the dark is lifting her head
rain is beginning to whisper
I remember the names of *things:*
dark   light
wind   water
laughter tears

But the names of my lovers
I cannot
I cannot remember

II
Acupuncture

Beyond the touch of a lover's fingers
upon my labia
are the sun's needles
probing deep
into the cunt
bestowing
divine heat

III
Blessing

Open or closed
my eyes possess the pattern
green oak leaves
vibrating branches

upon my veins
the veins of the tree
upon my ceiling
the garden's
wheeling bliss.

The Descent

I enter and am warm
in that dark cave
where mosses swarm
in slime on the rock wall
and water endlessly
registers no time

I have been in that place
of mucous and sweat
semen and swift blood
noon engendered
and I have seen
the toad's cold eye
and touched his coat
and pulled from my body
the after-birth

    (Most men
    cannot look on this
        and women shun
        bury the truth)

Yet I cry:
unless you have eaten
of this foul excreta
identified
and swallowed it
you are not whole
you are not man.

News from Nootka

For Louis Frank, Ahausit

They say the Tibetan monks came here
centuries past
wiped their feet on our shore –
In the roots of cedars
left silverware and prayers
walked into ocean
with incantations, ablutions
in praise of sunrise.

If it were all surmise
I'd be less shaken
than now, seeing you
strong, serene
priest of the cedars
figure emerging from argellite
sure-footed on the rock shore
launching canoes for fishing . . .
"When we had enough
we gave the rest to the village."

Something of how you were taken
into the troughs of the ocean
riding upon it alone
all night long
"in the dark a man is so small, so small"
Something about the spray shaken
out of your hair
and the calm brow
assure me now
the ancient messages endure:
"Receive me, O Maker of Morning
ready to act for my people."
Raven laid the sun in your lap:
your mind caught fire.

One Way Conversation

There are many men like you, perhaps
most certainly
most

but even though I've had
an itch for the seven-inch
reach   the hard entry
yet
I cannot despise you!

A woman wants above all
to be touched, caressed,
massaged and kissed
and what she carries away
the next day
is pride of flesh
love of link with man
human to human

O do not be distressed
that you cannot create
the great illusion:
thundering gods
at the womb's intrusion . . .
You have a role
valid as sunshine
of speech as equal
of man in parallel
pain . . . joy . . .
partner to woman
You have a role   gently caressing
human to human

Thumbing a Ride

I am the one who receives the many
cars coming at me:
I am the one
they are the many in familied boxes
flying for picnics
or in twos, man driving
woman slouched sleepwise

I am the one
glued standing
hand raised in a quick uncertain gesture
without a machine to run me
or animal to ride on
two legs for walking two eyes for talking
the sun sinking fast . . .
and beside this bare highway
only ditch grasses
bulrush frogsong
killdeer's grounded nest

I am the one desperate
to shout my predicament
passed by these hundreds
whizzing fast forward
to fixed destinations
I am unfixed
but glued to the highway
and even the killdeer
cries out against me
for invading his kingdom
his wings fluttering and feinting above me
his wings bring him home

I am the one
alone on the highway
language exists
in my thumb

Breathing

"You smell good
    you smell
as a woman should"

There have been eaters
    and drinkers of me
    painters of me
    eye bright
    and one singer
    who wreathed me
    in an aria

But I had yet to discover
    how even in old age
    a woman moves
    with freshness
is a leaf   perhaps
or a breath of wind
in a man's nostrils

Unitas

What happens to Allende
happens to you and me
who have not the courage
to take the knife, the gun
before that enemy
has girded on
his sinister plan:
we wait
for the plumb projected down
to fall in the well
and measure its level

What happens to our living
is death
to eating
is hunger
to crying
is silence

We, born to flourish
in a heyday of sun
and tumble to rubble
when the ice age comes.

The High

For Jason

On the sand
he whirled for five
six   seven   eight
ten minutes
oblivious
to calling come

turning alone
he whirled, a small
black cone
at the water's edge

"I was just trying to see
if a man really could take off
like a plane.
You don't believe it, do you, Gran?"

I believe!   I believe!

1975-1977

Les Anglais: Coming Out of Quebec

In the pitched dark
we wait on the siding
for the freight ahead
oncoming
Who will it bear
what Whitmanesque catalogue of goods
catapulting over
our hardrock country?

We are never told.
The slatted doors are tight-lipped
closed on a dark hold
and the wheels come clacking like tongues
talking alongside
in a foreign language
heading for action.
We lie strangers
locked in our own births
licking our own wounds
on the wrong side of knowledge.

1974

Reservations

Canada:
a necklace of isolates
a belt of bombas?

from here to here
from this campfire to that
St. John's Moosejaw Uclulet
how can we make out
together

only the Indians know
the secret of communication
a silent weeping
for the earth's
destruction

a silent gathering
of arms upraised
praising the air
we trample upon

I would give my little finger
and my thumb
if the giving
could make us
one

What would you give?
what fire steal
from what sun?

Who Are the Exiles

In the season of Indian Summer
when the Red, the Assiniboine
are showered with gold from the shore
images swaying yellow, spotlighting muddy waters
piercing the deep; fish transfixed by light

In the season of change, when a thousand suns
are shaken from a thousand trees
into the cracked skull of the land
to shelter dumb earth
from the next white, numbing invasion

In this their season
the people of the Ojibway are returning to the waters
they tread in silence the unbeaten paths
of the riverbank
they lie together at dawn in the hollows of leaves
praising the persistent sun
blazing October

And, in ones, separate, silent
I see them at the going down of the sun
sitting cross-legged, immobile
gazing across the golden river
to the world of silence

The people of the Ojibway have returned to their
        river
they drink of its molten liquid –

While above, on the heights we own
we huddle, white
enjoying the view
from our stony houses.

A Certain Dark

A dark has come down
a certain dark
friends move in fog
trying   trying
to mouth the right words
for the wry times.

Outside our window
a violet sky
broods over snowy river
and the cars prick their green eyes
scurrying over
      the arching bridge

It will be dark soon
a certain dark
never breathed before
by man or woman

Town Topics

Late fall afternoon on the rumbling street-corner
    hugging brown paper grocery bags
    we bump against each other
to argue
how can the artist live
in these times,
in these ruthless streets?
How can the good man
dipped in his own water
                                        colour
reflect the sky in his puddles?

How can the good woman
sewing a seam of words
display that whirling skirt
to the media-mesmerized
drugged eyes of the young
the aging young?

Will we ever see light again
tumbling down this tunnel?

Circumstantial Evidence

Even a candle
has this power,
the sun's –
can tear down
a town
or a totem

We move
shafted with accidents
random chances

Was it your face caught
then burned –
or was it
your mask?

I cannot see
                for crying
and
my glasses have vanished

Collared

My grandmothers, grand-aunts
grand cousins
always wore high lace
boned collars
around their necks –
and I always wondered why.

Today, in my sixties
I groan to see
the fingermarks of death
clutching my throat
and I know, now
the better wisdom of women:
to collar my neck
in a bright tie
or a chaste scarf
and hope I'm not too much noticed
by these young
eagle eyes.

The Takeover

Only at night, now
do we open the window
let in
the less polluted air

Only at midnight, now
is there some semblance of silence
machines shot into their stables
tails down   switches off

If we heard a horse, now, neighing
dog barking
owl hooting
lamb bleating
cock crowing
we'd clap hands to ears
"O what a fearful noise."

Even my voice
whispering   *love love*
vanishes
as the morning gallops up roaring
into its grinding machinations.

Conversation Macabre

Mostly we do
one quarter of what we would
or could
so frayed by demands –
that telephone!

Yet mostly
we are not hermits
gurus nor mystics
and cannot withdraw
into neutral bliss
to emerge pure
from the isolate tower.

How to find the recipe,
a just measurement?
or the equation,
power equal to power?

Every morning I awake, surprised
that you are not there
beside me
to defend your answers.

Ballad of the Battered Children

We have made a deal
have learned how to inhibit
the spiked dark:
we inhabit
blue utopias
wave
radiant rags of cloud

We are summoned
to the death cell
after the hangman
in the brown checked suit
rosy cheeks
silver hair
has sat with us at the judgment table
His children sit there too
listening to the judge
who is our father
cawing out words from the text in the Bible

The parents are in league
have judged us
to be the culprits
laying down our sins
for all to see
The parents have willed us
our death
the hangman rises, ready

But we have made a deal
with the powers of light!
Before their accusing fingers
their cursing cries
we vanish into
our blue horizon.

Book Review

For Pat Lowther

It was
that we did not know you enough
treasure your look enough
your casual word

It was
that we saw only the outer dress
the thin sharp bones, the skimpiness:
your presence that so lacked "show"
we took carelessly for granted.

It was as if
the fire burning in your eyes
failed to ignite ours

until now, facing your stones
we are blinded.

Life Styles

A city street
a corner
a nest
    is always
    over-peopled

but I accept
the situation
enjoy the tucked-in
kosher grocer
listen with silent laughter
to the sweet
private Hebrew lingo
demand
my buttermilk
my yogurt
FRESH!

I'm so lucky!
Can fly off
beside the rivering waters
cabined and closed
facing the sunset
that fans the fast-flowing
river,   Opposite
are the shivering yellow woods
sturdy   enduring

I'd like to think
we will never give up
the two life styles:
smell
of the teeming, jostling city
and life surrounded

by elms oaks   maples
harbouring blue jays and squirrels:
scent of earth   fast flowing water
gold drift of leaves –

I'd like to think
my grandchildren
would understand –
breathe hard –
seize onto these
two ways of being human.

Still Life

These fruits nestle
accept each other
touch   gently
in the golden bowl.

O might my thoughts so cluster
ever so gently
saying all
without breathing a word.

By the Same Author

Green Pitcher (1928)
Signpost (1932)
Day and Night (1944)
Poems for People (1947)
Call My People Home (1950)
New Poems (1955)
Selected Poems (1957)
The Colour of God's Face (1964)
The Unquiet Bed (1967)
The Documentaries (1968)
Plainsongs (1969,1971)
Collected Poems: The Two Seasons (1972)
Nine Poems of Farewell (1973)
Winnipeg Childhood (1973)
Ice Age (1975)
Right Hand Left Hand (1977)
The Woman I Am (1977)
The Raw Edges (1981)
The Phases of Love (1983)
Feeling the Worlds (1984)
The Self-Completing Tree (1986)
Les Âges de l'amour
(Translation by Jean Antonin Billard, 1989,
Governor General's Award)
The Husband (Prose, 1990)

Printed and bound
in Boucherville, Quebec, Canada by
MARC VEILLEUX IMPRIMEUR INC.
in September, 2000